The CEO of life? You!

Evincepub Publishing

Evincepub Publishing

Parijat Extension, Bilaspur, Chhattisgarh

First Published by Evincepub Publishing 2020

ISBN: 978-93-90362-55-4

The CEO of life? You!

By

Kiran Rk

About the Book

Humans are made up the way we think, by our thoughts. In life, things happen and things are going to happen. Every single human being on this earth feels all kinds of emotions – both negative and positive despite all the differences. But, how do certain people keep going and get better? How do certain people get the worse? The answer lies in the way we react to it.

A man knows happiness because he knows what sadness is. So, with this book, I want to share some things about life I've read, learned, and experienced with the group of people who are going through the same.

Life is a beautiful journey, but if we don't know how to walk, we are going to stumble.

Acknowledgement

The beginning is always the hard part. I never thought I would write a book about life. I never knew I have this side until I faced the chaos of life. So, one day I just grabbed my pen and paper, and now I'm writing the acknowledgment. First of all, I'm grateful to my family. To my father, R. K. Kheda and my mother R.K. Dayabati, my sisters R.K. Jina and R.K. Medhabati and my brothers-in-law, Syed Zaheer, W. Lakhikanta and my brothers R.K. Hemchandra and R.K. Rameshchandra. I wouldn't have written this if they hadn't supported me in everything I do.

To my best friends Bero, Deepa, Pite, Niki for always being there for me. Thank you, Dipak, Jackson, and Yohen for helping me with the cover. And special thanks to Linthoi Chanu. A big thanks to all my friends whom I haven't mentioned here.

And to my special someone with the prettiest smile, I'm glad that I've found someone so similar yet so different. To all the emotional rollercoaster that I went through, thank you for being with me.

Thank you, Hon, for adding more meaning to life. To the awesome night with the amazing people at the terrace, thank you Che Monika Khangembam and Mancy Khangembam.

Thanks to Rohitkanta Namram for the cover design.

Prakash, Vikram and the entire team at Evincepub publishing house.

Your Biggest Asset

Life Is What 10 per cent happens to you, and 90 per cent how you react to it.
-   Charles R. Swindoll

I was driving on the highway at full speed and turned on the car radio at its full volume listening to a guy talking about life. His voice was very calm and clear. But why do we listen to this? Why do we need to motivate ourselves every day? Is the guy on the radio born with these things? How does he learn about life? Or, is he reading some scripts? If yes, who actually wrote it? What made them write these? Who taught them about life? Are they actually applying the things to their real life? Are they really happy with their lives? I don't think so.

I think life is painful and it fucks every one of us, especially me. I can't recall the last time I laughed. I can't remember the time I felt loved. I don't remember the last time I was happy. The happiest moments of my life were being replaced with worry, anxiety, stress, and pain. I wanted to find peace, and was so tired of life, of people. I was just tired of everything. Then, I saw a truck coming in the opposite and I didn't slow down. My feet hit the accelerator harder than before and I was speeding so fast towards the truck. "Stop! Stop this moment!" the man on the tape raised his voice. No matter how much I wanted to end my life, I stopped. And I pulled over to the side of the road, every eye on the road was on me. I survived physically but my soul was already dead. It was a beautiful day, a beautiful evening. Afar, the sun was shielded behind the mountains, telling the world it was the end of the day. It left its beautiful bold colours across the sky. I looked up, and it was blue with a mix of different shades; it was clear like sparkling water. Just then, the clouds began to gather around. I wondered why they always kept moving. Why can't they stay still like I did? Like the tall, silent trees in front of the cliff edge I was sitting at. The wind was so gentle that day. Had a naughty blizzard been passing by, I would have fallen from the cliff; it would be okay if I fell. That was the moment I felt like shit because nothing was going right, everything was fucked up. I felt like bellowing my lungs out. At that moment, I needed a break from the world.

"Hey," a voice shouted.

I turned my back and it was Nathan my best friend. I smiled at him and turned knowing he was rushing towards me. I kept looking at the beautiful sight in front of me, ignoring the world.

"What the hell are you doing here?" his voice became clearer and louder.

"Come, sit with me. It's nice out here," I answered.

He came closer and looked for a seat, where the chances of falling were less. "Relax. We are not going to fall. If I'm falling, I'm taking you with me." I joked.

"You know some people say the moment you step onto the line between life and death, you feel everything; every tiny detail about life, you feel it." I continued.

Neither did he react to my bad-humoured joke nor did he reply to my words. I stared at the man sitting beside me and wondered how we turned out to be so different. When we were kids, we were always together; we were both happy and didn't have anything to worry about; we played until our eyes couldn't take it anymore; we cried when we didn't get what we wanted; we cried when we are hungry. But as we grew older, we split into two different people.

I remarked, "I don't know what happened to my life. I remember I was happy, sleeping in my mother's arm. My dad bought my birthday cake and I cried because he put my sister's name on it instead of mine. Life was simple back then. But now, everything is a mess. Family, friends, career, nothing is going right. I feel I'm choking up."

"Don't think too much," he said as he patted on my shoulder.

"It's easy for you to say. You have a great wife, a beautiful daughter, a great family. You drive a Mercedes, have money, and a good business. You and I are different." I said. I felt I was trying too hard to fit into the world; sitting beside a man like Nathan made me look like a complete loser. So, there was a cold atmosphere between us.

"Ah! It would have been be nice if we had some beer over here. If I knew you were not going to do something stupid, I might have stopped by and got some beer."

"You know, I thought about it." I smiled as I agreed.

Stunned, he said, "What? Jumping down the cliff? You are so stupid, man."

"It's because killing myself is the only solution I have. I have tried several times but it didn't work. I guess a part of me doesn't want to die yet. I remember once I jumped into a river and I didn't know how to swim; nobody was there, except for a friend. We had a small fight and I didn't know what to say or do, so I jumped. I was out of words and didn't know how to react; I just did it. I vividly remember that moment when my body touched the water surface; little by little, I started sinking. I heard my friend shouting and crying for help, but her voice started to fade away. The more I sank, the calmer her voice sounded. I started swallowing water and seeing things. It was then that I thought, 'This is how I'm supposed to die'. Then, I held onto something and realised if I would let go of it, that would be the end of my life. Part of me wanted to let go; that part wanted peace, to know if heaven and hell existed or not, the afterlife. He wanted to run away from the pain and misery of life. However, another part of me wanted to live. And, he won. I came out of water. I still don't know why I chose to hold on, I still wonder why I didn't give up."

"Sometimes, we question ourselves why are we living. Of billions living in this world, few find the answer. You know nothing is more valuable than your body, mind and soul," he reverted.

"My life is such a mess. I don't know how to live a happy life," I continued.

He replied, "The problem with you is the way you think - think big and be big, think small and be small, think positive and be positive, think negative and be negative, think good and good things will follow, think bad and everything will end up bad. It's up to you. Humans are made up by their thoughts, the way they think. You told me I have money, a great house, a Mercedes, a good business and all these assets. But to me, the biggest asset is my mind. Everything started from there and everything is going to end there. It is the most powerful weapon in the world; no nuclear energy can be more powerful than the mind. Earlier, you told me you were happy as a child. We all were happy when we were kids because the mind is all the same. We were positive despite the differences. Some are born with a silver spoon and some with rags, but we all were happy. So, when did we stop being happy? It was from the moment we got to know about the world. As we grew older, we started to feel these emotions – negative and positive. Fear, jealousy, greed, love, hatred, anger being some of these emotions. It's normal to feel these things. You might think successful people don't feel these things or feel only positive emotions. But the truth is, we all feel everything. We feel sad when we lose someone; we feel angry when we are betrayed; we are left heartbroken when we break-up with our partners; we feel terrible when someone talks behind our backs. So, the difference between you and me, the poor and the rich, the successful and unsuccessful is how we react to these emotions."

"Then, how am I supposed to react? How am I supposed to think?" I questioned.

"Heal yourself first. Only you can take care of yourself, no one else can do it for you. When you talked about killing yourself, I said 'it's stupid'. But it's understandable because I've been through that. So, when I hear that someone has killed himself/herself, I never question their reasons - one died of heartbreak, one because of family problem, another one because their career was not going straight, and so many reasons. When someone dies, you might have heard their families and friends blaming themselves, 'maybe, I should have been with her/him; maybe, I should have taken proper care of him/her; maybe I should have talked to him often'. But, nothing would change if they can't heal themselves. I remember when I was young, doing all these things and nothing was going right. I was really depressed. My wife – then my girlfriend – my family, friends, everyone was there with me but I was empty inside. I was full of anger, hatred, insecurities, jealously, and such negative emotions. My brother and sisters would call me every day to ask what I needed. Or, what I wanted to do? They reassured me time and again, or tried to talk me out by giving life lessons. My mom would cook my favourite meals, and my girlfriend was there when I needed someone to talk to. She got me an early edition of the book which I promised to read. But, no matter how hard they tried to help, it didn't change anything. I would feel better for a few minutes and a little later, it was all gone. I was disturbed with life and it affected the people around me. So, sometimes when it is too hard, I can understand why people kill themselves because they think it's the easiest option. When things like this happen, you might think it's crazy but I let a part of me float above leaving the other part a little lower. And, I can see everything – my family crying their hearts out, my girlfriend losing her mind and my friends punching the wall. Then, I realised that it might be easy for me but what about them? And, a few meters from there, I could see myself happy and successful surrounded by my people; just a few meters away from the happy place. So, I told myself, 'I need to heal'. I developed my own way of healing. I connected with nature. I would sit for hours looking at the trees and the birds; I would dump my negative emotions into the water day by day and it healed me," he enlightened me.

Further, he continued, "You should know about the things you can control and things you can't. You can't control somebody else's emotions, attitude, mind; so, why react negatively to it and feel bad about yourself? Let me tell you a story a friend of mine narrated: This friend of mine dated a girl for seven years and both their families knew each other. They planned their future together and it felt like they were meant for each other. But one day, the guy found out that his girlfriend was cheating on him with his best friend. He became depressed about it and tried hard to forget the whole thing. However, in the end, he killed himself. But, that girl is happily married today to his best friend and they have kids together; she has forgotten the guy as if he ever existed. So, whose loss was this? His mother is a broken-hearted woman and his father a crazy man. A similar thing happened to one of my employees as well; he told me this when having a drink. He once dated a girl, whom he loved dearly. But then things didn't work out well when she wanted more and left him. How did he take it? He became a better person. I know it's hard, and killing yourself is the easiest option; but why should someone kill themselves for someone who's cheating on them. Is he/she worth it? Of course, not. The one who cheated on you doesn't even deserve your love and you're going to kill yourself? See, I told you we can't control someone's behaviour or how they feel about us, but we can control ourselves, right? If someone did a bad thing to us, it doesn't mean we have to do the same. So, how do we deal with it? Let me give you an example. As we are talking about relationships right now, I'll talk about this. Let's say you are in a live-in relationship with your partner. At two in the morning, you get up from sleep for some water and find your partner is on the phone with someone else. You ask, "Who are you talking to, honey?" She/he answers, "A friend of mine." So, you get into bed and sleep. Again, some days later, it happens twice or thrice. You ask the same question and she/he answers the same thing. However, now, you have some insecurities, and have some doubts. So, this time you ask repeatedly after she/he hangs up. You don't have to shout, or take away their phone; just a few more questions. Positivity, I mean, doesn't always work? Isn't it? You might feel a little bit jealous; not that possessive-crazy-kind-of-guy. I mean where the spark in love is when there is no tiny amount of jealousy going on. Right girls? I don't mean to snatch your gf/bf phones or stalk them. I mean a little cute jealousy type. Maybe, a friend was going through a break-up or something, and that's why they are calling at odd hours since they need help. You don't know that, yet you should ask. And if she/he is cheating on you, then that's the end of the story. You don't have to throw a tantrum. Maybe, he/she is not satisfied with your relationship or maybe he/she is someone who doesn't deserve you. So, whatever situation you are in, it's okay to feel these things. It's okay to feel a bit of jealousy. But as I told you before, the way you react to it is going to make the change. Such things come with pain and are natural; everyone feels it. Sometimes, we feel like we are falling in a pit and feel like we can't get out of it. But for people like us – we always fall into the pit yet come out with something else in our hands; we take advantage of the pain. We know we might fall into it again because it's life; so, we learn how to get out of it. We believe in 'if life gives you a lemon, squeeze it hard and throw it back to the world'. We don't stand still; we don't keep quiet; we rise from any kind of pain."

I quickly rebutted, "See, we are in a different situation. You have the most faithful and beautiful wife on the planet; you don't have anything to worry about your relationship. You have a beautiful daughter, who is the sweetest kid I know. If you've lost millions in business, you still have billions left; it's easy for you to get out of that pit. You have nothing that causes you pain. How would you know about it? How can you relate to my feelings?"

He smiled at me and answered, "We both have the same family background. Today, I'm successful but you are not. I knew if a man wanted something, he could get it; you didn't know this. I didn't give up but you gave up. For example, if I was in your position, I wouldn't be sitting here or run away from anything. Success, health, happiness, wealth, how do you think I got it all? I got it because I went through everything and faced every obstacle I met. If you run away from pain, misery, the hardships, then you are repelling the wealth, happiness as well as a successful life. Your negative attitude is repelling the good things in life."

"Well, enough for now. Let's go. It's getting late," he quipped.

"But, I like it here," I answered.

"Yes, but this is your escape. We have to go back to reality." he said.

With a heavy sigh, I got up.

He got into his Mercedes and waved goodbye. I got into mine – the old Hyundai. My best friend looked sharp with his clear haircut and trimmed beard; wearing a suit and watch I dreamt of. And, there was me with my old Casio trying to make ends meet and driving a car ready to break down at any second. I was surprised I drove that car all the way up till there. I fought with the gear, and the old clutch made it harder; I used all the little energy left in my body to win the gear battle. Then, the car behind me started honking loudly as if he was carrying a VIP.

At first, I didn't pay any attention to him as I was busy with the gear battle. He started honking continuously and that annoyed me; so, I gnarled at him from my window, "Shut the fuck up."

He left me and my cranky car behind shouting some swear words as well. As I looked at the speedometer, I realized I was driving very slow. Maybe, because my car was not in the working condition or maybe, because I didn't want to reach home. Then, I saw an interesting sight – a girl and a boy on a bike. The girl was hitting on the boy and laughing; it looked like they were in love. That reminded me of my younger days. Time changed so fast, I thought to myself.

With all the mixed feelings, I drove back to my empty apartment. It has been years since I moved out of my parent's house. We all lived together like one big family – my parents, brothers, our dog and I. However, I felt so suffocated in the house that I left. I rented a small apartment and that's how I ended up at this place. The car I was driving was my father's; they bought a new one; so, I was using the old one. I took out my worn-out jacket and left it on the chair which was wearing all the clothes I owned. I took out my shoes and jumped straight onto my bed. No one called to ask whether I had food or not. No one asked how I was handling life. Nobody cared if I existed or not. I was all alone in this world.

The Wise Guru

A negative mind will give you a negative life.

It was a Sunday morning. I got up late than usual. I wanted to have some home-cooked food that morning because it was long that I've been surviving on instant noodles, coffee; at the office, my drawer was full of restaurant flyers and my belly was a proof. So, I decided to cook a nice meal for myself. But then, when I opened the fridge, BAM! nothing was inside except for the box of chocolates someone had gifted last winter and some sauce sachets. And, the sink smelled like shit. With an empty fridge and an empty wallet, it turned into a cleaning day instead. As I was cleaning and organizing the tables, I found a book – an interesting book. It was introduced to me by someone whom I'm not sure if I'm close enough to call a friend. He was my classmate, but we never had a real conversation in school. He was just a mediocre man back then. So, I met him coincidentally some years ago and I was taken aback. His company was growing when I met him, and recently his company was featured on the cover of a business magazine with him standing next to the logo. That guy, who didn't even know how to stand in front of the camera, was now posing like a pro. A guy with average grades was a millionaire. So, when I met him back then, I jokingly asked him if he's into some kind of black art or magic or did he recently find that his father is secretly wealthy? His answer was the Law of attraction.

"Wow! Someone's cleaning up. Nice." I was startled by the sound from behind.

"How the hell did you get in here?" I asked Nathan.

"Please! Your door is open, sir. I entered through it," he answered in a cocky way.

"I didn't know you read books. Which one is that?" He asked as he noticed the book in my hand.

"Ah! The Law of Attraction? The subconscious mind. It's a good book. Have you read it?"

"I've read half of it and it didn't work."

"Why did you stop reading the book halfway? You are saying it didn't work for you, so how did you try?" he continued asking.

"Well, I was excited when I first heard about the Law of Attraction. It's so funny I even tried doing that. I remember the first morning I read the book. I was visualizing things and picturing these perfect mental images of me driving a Mercedes wearing a suit. I was picturing myself with the number of digits on my bank account and was repeating to myself 'yes, I'm a happy successful man' hundreds of times, but after a week or so it wasn't fruitful to me so I stopped."

He burst out laughing and said, "Dude, what happened to that 'Rome wasn't built in a day?' Do you think it's going to happen overnight? Halfway reading just one book, or watching a 10-minutes video, and you will become successful overnight? That's the stupidest thing I've ever heard."

"But, I was doing exactly what he taught me and what the book told me. I believed in myself, but nothing changed in me."

His smile was gone at that instant, and he looked straight into my eyes and said, "I've told you that the mind is the most powerful weapon in the world, right? It can do anything, literally anything. The law of attraction is not some kind of voodoo art or some superstitious beliefs or some bullshit. Well, in the books, it says you want to listen to the radio. Let's say, you have to tune in to a particular frequency. For us, if we want to listen to the FM channel, we have to tune it to 103.5 MHz. If not, then we might not be able to hear the radio. If we want the good things in life, we have to make sure we tune into the same frequency. So, if you don't believe in yourself that you can do it, if you don't believe in yourself that you can't tune the particular frequency, then I'm sorry. It is nothing but a belief in yourself. That's how the law of attraction works for me."

Suzy Kassem said, "The doubts kills more dreams than failure ever will." If you are having doubts about yourself, then I'm sorry you can't do anything in life.

YOU HAVE TO BELIEVE IN YOURSELF!'

"Okay. Let's say your room is next to a dumpster. Imagine it's a pleasant morning, you get up feeling good and you have this energy to start the day. You go to the kitchen, make yourself a nice cup of tea and want to enjoy it with the view. So, you open your window and 'DAMN IT! EVERYTHING IS GONE AT THAT INSTANT!' Because of the smell from the dumpster. So, the next day you throw some fresh flowers, which smell the sweetest on the dumpster. Do you think it's going to smell different?"

"No, right? Because the shit is still there. So, you have to clear that first; it's not an overnight job, right? The same is with your mind. You have to clear out the negative things, if you want a good smell. You have to learn how to master your emotions. The thoughts alone are not enough to have results. You need actions, too, to get the desired result. See, I told you, it's all in the mind. The mind has three parts – the conscious, the unconscious, and the subconscious. The mischievous, craziest and the most powerful part is the subconscious. It can do anything. Just tell your subconscious mind you want this, and it will think of a way how to get it. Believe me, the subconscious mind works in different ways. If you want happiness, just sow the happy seeds in your subconscious mind and you'll be happy. *Sebot tharaga Mairen panba hounade.* So, don't sow seeds that are going to make you unhappy. Throw it out or else it is going to grow. If you want money, your financial intelligence will wake up. If you want to love, you will find love. You know the word, *Chindung Inba* (if you say something bad or good, it is going to happen to you), right? We all believe this theory but few know how it works. This is your subconscious doing the job. It doesn't know whether you are joking or you want something to happen. Though our subconscious mind is like a wise Guru, it doesn't understand jokes. I'll tell you some stories and you can relate to it. Remember when we were kids, all went for *Nakatheng* (In Manipur, there's a festival called Yaoshang. On the evening of the first day, and the morning of the second day, all the boys are dressed up and girls wear the traditional dresses; the kids go to the neighboring houses and the elders give them coins.) So, everyone told me to wake up early in the morning for the second day. I had a problem waking up early when I was a kid. So, I told them I can't. Then, one of them said, 'Don't worry about that. Just ask your pillow to wake you up at 5 am, hit it three times and go to sleep. Don't open your eyes after that.' So, I believed him and did it. Guess what? I got up exactly at 5 am. I didn't know how it happened until 20 years later, when I realized it was the subconscious doing the job. They told me not to open my eyes after saying those words, it was because the subconscious mind is active mostly either when we begin to sleep or the moment after we just wake up. So, if I opened my eyes after that, my mind would see things and my mind won't concentrate on waking up at 5 am. That's how I did it. And, another one is what my grandmother always said day and night, '*Esor Ibungo sidoi oiradi nongta naraga sijage.*' One day, she was just fine, doing her routine and we had the evening tea and snacks. Later that evening, she had a pain in her chest. She was taken to the hospital, but she can't make it. She died that day. We didn't know how her words turned into reality, but it was her subconscious mind that took her life. She sowed it in her subconscious that if she fell sick, she was going to die that moment. So, when she was at the hospital bed, when she knew she was sick, she gave up on herself. Please trust your subconscious mind. Use it for the good cause. Every successful person uses it. It's not a joke. You know when I started my own business, I didn't have beautiful paintings or pictures on the wall. All I had were writings on small pieces of paper and glued them to the wall. Whenever I would go to sleep or I wake up, they were all there. I wrote down things about positivity, the theories, about business and all which I found in books, online classes, and which I heard from people all over the wall. And on the nearest wall, next to my bed, I had written what I would achieve in the next month or the next year or when I'm 30 or 40. And what I would do about my business, about my big plans and all these things. I saw it every day when I was in my room. When I woke up and when I went to sleep. And, it's really helpful because we have thousands of thoughts going inside our head every second, every minute, every day. So, the subconscious mind is not sure which one we want in life. But if you are seeing the words repeatedly, the subconscious mind takes it and processes it."

"Well, I haven't thought about it that much." I told him.

"Dude. I DON'T KNOW ABOUT MAGIC, BUT THIS DOES WORK," he whispered.

Why is God Taking Sides?

Nobody told you it's impossible, it was your own thought.

"Come on. I'm hungry. Let's get downstairs and eat something," I said.

"We can cook something here," he replied.

"I don't have anything to cook," I replied while grabbing a shirt from the chair.

As we continued walking, people kept staring at him for his young looks, tall figure, expensive clothes and an expensive watch. And then, people looked at my dark eyes and unshaved face with messy hair. I looked like a homeless bum, wearing cheap worn-out clothes and a fat belly. They looked at me with disappointment. They must be thinking how these two people are walking together. Or, was I overthinking? Just then, an extreme honking began. People looked frustrated at the traffic. The rush hour had begun.

"Today is Sunday, right?" I asked.

"Yeah."

"Look at the traffic! It's Sunday, people! Get some rest for god sake," I shouted in the open.

"I like cities that never sleep, you know. Well, for the weekends, I want to go to a quiet place and enjoy myself with my family. But, other days, I like exploring new cities. The crowded ones, especially. I like the rush, the energy, the people, their food, their roads, their gods. I like it," he said.

"So, you believe in god?" I asked

"What do you think?"

"Well, for a guy like you, I don't think so. You are an atheist, aren't you?"

"What about you? Do you believe in god?" he asked me.

"I don't think so. I used to believe in him and prayed to him every day. But, he never answered my prayers. If there is god, I think he only answers to the rich and the successful people, I guess. God doesn't answer our prayers."

He answered calmly. "When I was a little younger, I remember one afternoon. My mother was making a lot of incense sticks and I was sitting beside her enjoying my book. Then, my mom, exhausted from making them, told me, 'I'm getting tired.' I replied, 'Why don't you buy them?' To that, she answered, 'The ones available at the market have uneven tips and don't fit the stand. Besides, we use nearly 20 incense sticks every day. So, I better make these myself.'

That day I asked myself a series of questions. Why are we praying twice a day? Why are we using incense sticks and candles? Why do we need to take a bath before praying? I mean, when we pray in a bad situation, we don't really care if we have taken a bath or not. I thought a lot about all of these. And, like you said, that god only grant wishes to the rich, my mom also used to say that. The prayers gets answered for some people and not for others.

And my answer to your question is that I'm not an atheist, but I hate the idea of believing 100 per cent in god. When I started the restaurant, I had a hard time in the first two months. The sales were so low. So, my mother came up to the restaurant in the morning and prayed to the little poster of a god at the corner. She couldn't do that often as she had to climb a flight of stairs. The funny thing was if she did that, the sale would be high or average but not low. She thought it was her doing and that god made the sales. But, I thought it was my idea of positivity that made the sales. Whether the sales were going up because of my mother's belief or mine, it was going the right way. My point is, people have different beliefs and it's ok if you believe in a different god. It's ok if you don't believe in a god. My mother believes in her god and that made the sales. For me, my subconscious mind made the sales. So, to me, whatever we believe in, that's our god right there.

I don't know whether god exists or not, but some part of me believes in him in accordance with the situation. When I see an ambulance driving at a full speed, I pray for him/her to God. Because there is nothing I can do, I leave it to god. When the whole world was dying because of the COVID-19, I prayed to god. Well, I did my part by taking the precautions, social distancing norms, and the things I could; they were just for me and my family. There was nothing I can do to help the people who were already affected. In this kind of a situation, I prayed to God. I prayed if someone could just find a cure so that everything could be back to normal and people could be back to their family and loved ones. I prayed that people would stop dying. And if I want something materialistic, let's say a car, I don't pray to god. I pray to my subconscious mind. When we are praying, we are murmuring those words to ourselves. It's a good thing we take a bath before praying, so our mind and body are fresh. And to me, the dim light of the candles and sweet scent of incense sticks really helps in making a serene environment for praying to self. Normally, we pray twice, right? In the morning and evening. That's a good thing, because we have around 60,000 thoughts every day and our mind doesn't know which ones to process. So, you keep repeating the things you want, and the subconscious mind will know it. You told me you never get what you want; do you know why?

Let me tell you a story. There was a man, who was born in a middle-class family. He worked at a private firm and earned an average salary. Despite being the sole earner of the family, he also dreamt of owning a Rolls Royce someday. So, every morning he would get up early, take a bath, and pray to the god in the corner. Later in the evening, he would do the same. And his Rolls Royce was with him in every prayer. After years and years of the same routine, nothing changed. He thought, 'maybe I should pray harder or maybe I should go to the temple where everyone is going'. So, on the weekends, he would visit the famous temples and pray the exact same thing. Again, it wasn't fruitful to him. Later, he decided to stop praying because he thought God was taking sides. So, what went wrong: Yes he prayed every day; but after minutes of praying, when he was having lunch with dal and rice, he knew it was almost impossible to get a Rolls Royce in that state. Nobody told him it's impossible, it was his own thought. So, in the 24 hours, he thought of owning the car for 10 minutes and the rest of the time, he thought that he couldn't. That's why he didn't get it, no matter how many times he prayed. So, when you pray, leave the negative thoughts behind. See, the subconscious mind can't do multitasking. It is supposed to work on the thoughts you think. If you mix up the negative with the positive thoughts, the subconscious mind gets confused. So, you won't get what you want, no matter how many times you pray. So, when somebody asked me about the restaurant, 'How are the sales?' I always responded, 'the sales are good' even if I was hardly making any. I replied that way because I don't want my subconscious mind to get confused. If I'm praying or wishing for the sales to improve and if I'm answering, 'Well, the sales are no good or it's the worse!', I'm giving contradictory thoughts to my subconscious mind and the worst will happen. If I'm replying, 'it's good', I'm convincing my subconscious mind that the sales are good and want it to affirm that the sales are going up.

Your old Hyundai or the red Mercedes?

Once you replace the negative thoughts with positive ones, you'll start having positive results.

-   Willie Nelson

My phone started beeping, so I checked excitedly to see whose name popped up. It had been long I heard that tone.

"Wake up. It's almost 4.30 am," I called up Daisy, my girlfriend.

"Okay. I'll get ready," she answered in a mumbled tone.

It was winter, and it was still dark when I went to pick her up. The street lamps were on and there were few people on the streets. She came out wearing layers of clothes and looked cute. I liked the way how she looked. We drove 40 km from the city up to a resort and walked a few steps towards their sightseeing area. Nobody was there since it was early in the morning and it was cold. We sat on a bench, which had a clear view of a beautiful lake. We saw the fishermen trying to get on their boats and assembling the nets from afar. The birds sitting on the tall trees were singing different tunes. I looked at the beautiful woman I loved sitting beside me; her hair falling down her soft cheeks. When I stared into those brown eyes, I saw the reflection of the rising sun. Everything about that moment, it was my definition of perfection.

Then, the phone beeped and it turned out to be the landlord. I had delayed rent by five days. Damn it! I left my phone and got up to get some water; it beeped again when I came back. With a little hope that someone I know cared for me, I checked again. Again, it was not good news. It was my employee, who was not coming to work the next day. Now my "fuck-it level" rose to 100. I had 10 employees at the beginning, but after the business started to decline slowly, one by one, they all started quitting because I could not pay them well. They all quit, except for this guy who texted me and another one. And he was not coming tomorrow. So, this was it, I thought. How am I supposed to think positive thoughts at a time like this? How am I supposed to stay positive when the whole world was eating me alive? I was so frustrated at myself, and with everyone around me. I was frustrated at the world. So, I went downstairs and walked the quiet street. I saw the street dogs lying in front of the closed shops. I wondered if they ate or not. Forget about one dinner; did they eat at all during the whole day? What happened yesterday or the day before? Who's feeding them? One can look into their eyes and know if they are hungry or not. They can't speak; they can't say anything – whether they are hungry or not – but for us humans, we can work for food. We could ask someone for help. We can say what we want, what we need. We are lucky to be born as a human being and yet we take this for granted. So, I calmed myself. But, I needed alcohol; so, I bought the cheapest alcohol I could get. I used to drink whiskey worth thousands when my business was doing well, but for now, I bought the cheapest. It would help me get some sleep. I reached my apartment and went straight to bed. I sat there and drank half of it neat. I dreamt of a dark quiet town, but did not remember how I had reached there. I didn't see anyone and started walking down the streets. I was parched as a desert. So, I searched for a place to get some water and my body started sweating as I walked. Soon, I saw a big lake at a distance and I tried hard to reach there. Out of nowhere, a pack of wolves were staring at me with their hungry eyes and I started running away from them as fast as I could. As I took a turn, two cars were parked parallelly – my old Hyundai and Nathan's red Mercedes.

Then, the soft strumming of guitar from my phone startled me. I was sweating profusely. And, my heart was pounding so fast that I was shaking.

"Are you up?" asked Nathan on the other end of the phone.

"Yeah. Dude, I saw your car in my dream." And, I told him all about my dream.

"Sometimes, the positive thoughts don't work. You told me not to think about the negative thoughts as they would grow up but I can't," I continued.

He ignored my last words and asked, "Which car did you get in?"

"Yours, I guess. But, my dream wasn't vivid. Your call woke me up," I replied.

"You chose the Mercedes because you want to get away from the wolves, right? So, you agree that my car runs faster than your old car, right?" he asked.

"Is that even a question? Yeah-huh!"

"Well, I told you to think only positive thoughts. But, the mind is very cunning in a way. If you keep forcing yourself to think about the positive things only, the mind is going to do the opposite. It is going to think only about the negative thoughts. We cannot stay positive all the time, I agree. It's normal to think about the negative thoughts. You are having the negative thoughts not be because you want them. We, human beings, want to live a normal peaceful life without any complications. But, things happen to us and they are going to happen. Your mind is auto-suggesting a negative thought because of the situation you were in. Everyone has flaws, makes mistakes. Every day, we are being chased by the wolves of reality. And, we can't get away from them. We can't control certain situations, so we have to learn how to deal with them. Can you stop thinking about the negative thoughts? No, it's going to be hard. But can you think of any positive thought? Yeah, you can. So, do it. But first admit it to yourself that, it is wrong. Admit that you're thinking a bad thought and you want to change it."

"When I met my wife, we had a rough start. Both of us were a mess when we met each other. I was just spiraling around with my career, family, love life, friends – the baggage of life. And, she was doing the exact same thing. So, we fought a lot. A friend said 'if she had a dollar for every time we fought, she'd be rich by now'. We even questioned ourselves if we were compatible or not. That led to a series of questions on the back of our minds. So, we were chased by our own wolves, by our own negative thoughts. One night I told her, 'I think I'm falling deeper in love with you day by day.'

She said, 'Don't.' Because she thought if it didn't work out, it would hurt us really bad.

Then, I answered, 'I know we are chased by the negative thoughts and it is impossible not to think about it. But, don't tell me to stop when I say I'm falling deeper in love because we need a powerful thought if we want to survive. And, in our case, we have love. So, don't worry about anything as long as we have strong feelings for each other. The negative thoughts can be suppressed by a more powerful thought.'

You can't run away fast with your busted car, right? The wolves can easily outrun you while you are fighting with the gear. If you get into your busted car, you are going to die. You need my Mercedes if you want to survive. So, every time, you think of a negative thought, at that instant, think of a more powerful positive thought. My Mercedes can easily suppress your busted car, right? Like that, the negative thoughts can be suppressed by your more powerful positive thoughts as well."

The Worrier Princess

Worry never robs tomorrow of its sorrow, it only saps today of its joy.

-Leo Buscaglia

That morning, I was shivering when I woke up. It was raining heavily outside and I was feeling really cold as I was only in my boxers. No one would dare to go out, but I couldn't resist the weather. I find peace when it rains, and it kind of soothes my soul. So, I grabbed a shirt and a pant and got down to get some hot coffee and something to eat from the local shop.

"Hey?" a man with half-soaked clothes called.

I turned my back and it was a friend from college. "Hey, what are you doing here? It's good to see you," and gave him a two Mississippi hug.

"I'm waiting for the rain to stop. Come sit here with me."

'So, how are you doing?" I asked.

"I'm good. I just had a baby recently. So, are you married? How's your work?"

"What the fuck man! Easy tiger, easy! I just met you for a minute after seven years and all these questions!" I thought to myself but I just replied, "I'm fine."

"Oh, by the way, I just heard yesterday that Toby has cancer," he told me with his eyes wide open.

"Really?" I was shocked.

"Yeah, and you know he doesn't have a strong financial support. So, I feel bad for him," he murmured.

I felt really bummed out. I woke up feeling a little good because it was raining, and it was all ruined. I was thinking about Toby all the way up to my apartment. I guess it wasn't just about him. I was also thinking about my life. Everyone I knew was settling down, having kids, earning enough and was happy. What about me? What if something happens to me like Toby? I felt like killing myself because thoughts were worrying me. So, the next moment, I grabbed my car keys and ran downstairs as fast as I could. I knew where I was going. I looked up to the sky and the dark clouds were moving towards me. The street looked the same, except there were more umbrellas. The sound of the engines running, the horns, the people, they were all buzzing like angry bees. As soon as I hit the road, the rain began slowing down and came to stop as I reached the place. It gave me a warm and cozy feeling when I entered the place. I walked the pathway and could feel the earthy smell of the freshly cut grass on the lawn. I rang the doorbell.

"What a pleasant surprise," Nathan greeted me.

I faked a smile like I usually did.

His wife came out with a bum in her stomach. "Hi! It's been so long. Come inside."

Their living room was quite spacious and we sat on the couch. Just then, "Look who's here?" Nathan said to his daughter, who came out of the room with a teddy.

"Wow, you've grown so much. Come here," I tried to hold her but she turned to her dad and hid her face.

"She's shy. Wait for a few minutes and she will turn you upside down," Nathan smiled and said to me holding his baby.

"So, another one?" I asked.

"Yeah, we wanted to have a quartet family so."

"Is there something you want to talk to me about?" he continued.

"Not much. I was just tired of being alone. I needed someone, so I came."

"It means so much that you remembered me when you needed someone," he said.

"I met a friend from college this morning and he was asking about settling down, this and that, and how a friend got cancer. It was a lot to take in one moment. I mean I've got enough problems to worry about."

"Worrying is the thing that's killing us. It is the thing that's making one's life miserable, if we don't know how to deal with it. If we overthink our worries or if we focus on it, we might not be able to live. That's when depression hits, health problems start, and so on," he remarked.

"Don't you have any worries?" I asked

He burst out laughing, "I'm a human being dude."

"But how do you deal with this?" I reiterated.

Just then his wife came in with tea in her hands.

"Why? You don't have to do this. I hope it's not too much trouble for you," I said, as Nathan helped her putting the tea on the table.

"No, no. Try it! It's locally made."

Nathan thanked his wife with a smile and she left the room.

"One day, as I was walking down the street, I saw birds sitting on the spire of one building, but none of them sat on the nearby buildings. I wondered why? Because that particular building had a place for the birds to sit. You are worrying about something because you have space and time for that in your mind. You know my wife would overwork herself, if something is bothering her. There are two types of worries. The first one is about the reality you are facing right now. I mean, let's say, when you are having a problem with your work or family. For this, you can't ignore it. You have to face it. You have to put it down on your table and sort it out. What are you worrying about? Find out the answer and think about how to solve it; hundreds of ideas will come running to you about how to solve what is worrying you. If you ask yourself that question, the answer will come out. Why most of the people get worried all the time is because they don't ask that question. There's a famous saying that if you want something, ask yourself how you can get it? If you ask how, the answer will come. And if you don't ask yourself and just conclude that you can't get it, your mind will shut off."

"The second type of worry happens to someone who overthinks a lot. When you are worried about your friends getting married and having kids, you look at yourself and feel scared about life. If we think, or if we see someone's mother dying, or if you think that your parents are going to die someday, you start imagining your life without them; or, if you see a video on Facebook about someone's dog dying, you start imagining about your dog – it hurts you like hell. We never know what's going to happen to you or your friends or your loved ones. If you keep thinking about these, you can't get up. Also, you can't stop worrying about it because you know it's going to happen someday. When you see your colleague getting fired from his job, you start worrying whether you might be next. Or, when you hear that your friend has cancer and you start worrying if the same thing happens to you. These are the things not happening to you right now, but you keep worrying about these. How can you get rid of these?"

"So, there is this place I usually go out to have some alone time. It's actually a footpath – a wide one –

and it has trees and benches. One faces this great view of a lake and an old palace. The footpath is clean, except for the dry leaves falling from the big beautiful trees. And, its edges are fenced by cement railings. It is a beautiful place, but a little below the railings, there's a lot of trash such as empty bottles, packets, and everything. The problem with that area is that it is hard to clean and you can't use sweepers as the gap is very small. The only solution is to get it out one by one using the hands. That, too, won't be easy. My point is life is like this. You see certain things but you can't clean up the mess. You feel things but you can't do anything about it. But, it's up to you whether you want to focus on the dumpster or the great view of the beautiful trees, the old palace, and the lake. You can choose. Instead of worrying about the future, just focus on your present. Everyone around having kids doesn't mean you should have one. It's about one's timing. Instead of thinking about your parents dying or your dog dying, try to live the moment with them. You won't have any regrets; after all, we all are mortals. Instead of worrying about getting fired from your job, do the best you can. Instead of worrying about having cancer, just take precautions such as your diet, health, exercise. Live every day like it's your last day."

Failure doesn't mean you've made the wrong choice

We may encounter defeats, but we must not be defeated.

-Maya Angelou

"Wake up dude. Wake up. You there?" a voice on the door woke me up.

I looked at my phone and it showed 4 a.m.

"Who the hell is at my door at this hour?" I thought.

"Can you hear me?" the familiar voice continued shouting. I slowly tried to gather myself up and walked out.

"What the fuck man? What happened?" Nathan, looking fresh and active, stood outside.

"Come, let's go for jogging," he said.

"No, I want to sleep. It's still dark. Go away," I told him, as I tried closing the door.

"Nope, we have to go," he insisted on walking.

"It's too early. I'm perfectly healthy. So, I don't have to jog," I said, trying to get back to sleep.

He ignored what I said and continued looking for my shoes. "Where the hell did you keep your shoes? Let's go."

I replied, "I'm not going."

He kept looking, until he found it under the chair. Then, he pulled off my blanket and said, "Put these on."

Knowing he will keep doing that, I got up reluctantly.

"Yes, that's the spirit. Come on let's go," he said, walking out of the door excitedly. I followed him with the little energy I had. So, we started jogging for a few minutes and I started puffing with sweat. Looking at the poor sweaty guy, my best friend laughed at me, "You told me you are perfectly healthy. What happened to you?"

"No, it's just that it's been so long I ran like this. So, my body isn't accepting it," I told him, as I slowed down.

"Fine. We'll walk then," he said.

"How come you have a lot of energy at this hour?" I queried.

"I'm always like this every morning. So, what time are you going to work?" he asked.

"No. we are not going to open today."

"What happened?"

"Nothing. One of my employees is not coming to work for a few days. So, we can't open without him."

He looked surprised and added, "One of your employees is not coming to work and you are going to close the entire day? If he suddenly dies, then your business will also shut down?"

"It's not that. I've only two staff left. So, we can't function properly with only one," I replied.

"You can hire an extra employee for the day or can work twice. You can't do anything with that attitude man," he commented.

"Sometimes, I think I've made the wrong decision. Maybe, I should find a job with my degree. I don't have to worry about anything; I'll get paid every month," I said.

"If you want to do it, you can. But let me ask you this: What makes you want to do this? Why didn't you look for a job earlier when you had just got your degree? What makes you think that you've taken the wrong decision?" he enquired.

"Well, first of all, I had no hope for government jobs because they sell their jobs. I heard they charge a lot even for a fourth-grade job. I don't have any eye witness or anything, but it's a known fact. And secondly, I didn't want to work for private companies paying 7,000-8,000 a month. It's not just about the low pay; I thought I might get tired of the people using all my energy with that little amount. Also, the thing that scares me the most is doing the same thing over and over again. So, the best option I had was to start something of my own."

"Then, why are you regretting it? You are doing what you want, right?"

"Yes. But, I'm tired of it. I'm in debt. Everything is eating me alive. My business is not doing good. I feel like quitting it. Every month, every year, I thought it was going up; it's getting worse step by step, year by year."

"Dude, you are just shouting 'I'm sinking. I'm sinking' sitting on a boat with a hole. You just can't sit still waiting to sink. Instead, you can try to cover it up with something or row faster or maybe you can try to break a piece of it and carry yourself to a nearby island. It may sound impossible to you, but at least you should try. Sitting quietly and waiting for the boat to sink or trying different things – which one has a better chance to keep you alive? Okay, forget about this whole thing. Let's say if someone gives you a job offer, will you do it?"

"I might because I'm in huge debt."

"You think you can work, even though you hate it, to be out of debt? Mark my words; you'll get into depression within a month," he told me.

"But, I don't think I know what I'm doing."

"Then, learn about it. You see there are two kinds of people in the world. One kind wants to do something, they want to do what they are good at. So, I met this guy who came to my restaurant with a friend. He was a little older than me – four to five years. We talked about start-ups and he told me, 'I want to open something like this, something unique. But, I don't want to do if I'm not good at.' Well, I know what he meant and it's a good thought. The other kind of people are my type. If it is something I want to do, even though I'm not good at it, I will do it. I might lose some money at first, but I think of it as my learning fee. And I'll do well in that field. After two months of opening my restaurant, the chef had a family accident and couldn't come to the café; she was the only chef I had. So, the urgent hunt for the chef went on; it was not easy. Luckily, we found one, but would come in two months. So, we are 60 days without a chef. I thought about closing it for a few months, but my mom told me not to as we'll lose our regular customers. So, I opened with the thought that we'll serve the easy ones and if they order something complicated, I'll apologize sincerely. But, nothing is complicated if you think you can do it. The first day went well as the customers ordered the easy stuff. On the second day, they ordered Chinese and I made it. I cooked everything on the menu for those 60 days. So, my point is – the first kind is good but the second kind are even better because you can do whatever you want and you'll excel in that field. Nobody is born with talents. You learn first and become a master in that field; the second kind of people have it. It is never too late to learn anything. So, if you feel like you want to shift to another thing, you can but do it only if you want to. Not because you didn't know anything about the first one. Read lots of books, join seminars maybe online classes if you don't have time, talk to people who are already doing what you want to do. You'll learn a lot. It's okay if you don't know the way. Look at people who know it, and ask them for directions or follow them. When I say follow them, I don't mean you should imitate the way they walk. Just ask for the directions and walk. Let's say there is a boy who is a music prodigy. He started playing the guitar when he was just a year old. But someone had to be there for him to teach how to hold the guitar properly, how to use the fingers, the finger exercises, the chords, etc. That is what I mean by asking for directions. After the child knows the basic things, he'll play a solo of his own. That's what I mean by walking your own. We've seen a lot of actors and singers, trying to be just like their mentor or someone they love but what happened to them? They don't have their own way now. So, don't try to walk exactly like them. There's a saying: If you want to be creative, then abstain from imitating."

"See, for now, I don't have anything left. As if I have no choice. I feel like this is it. I'm not in the place to start again," I told him.

"Hold on a second," he stopped walking and said, "Look at me! Do you think I didn't have a down moment like you do? Forget about me. Look around, all famous people – writers, singers, actors, entrepreneurs, artists. Take a good look at their history; they all failed at a certain point. It's not like they had a beautiful voice, a great idea, they started doing it and succeeded at the first try. No, it doesn't work that way. Almost every famous people on the Earth failed – not once, but hundreds of times. There's a story behind every great person. Like I said before, we also feel everything. We have also had our fair share of failures. But, they made a record of the history. How? That's because we know the meaning of 'temporary defeat'; temporary means lasting for a short period. But people like you get confused with the permanent and give up easily. Richard Nixon said, "A man is not finished when he is defeated. He is finished when he quits". Thomas Edison had one thousand unsuccessful attempts. If he had quit at the first two-three attempts, we might not have had the electric bulb. A great plan needs a great mind. To achieve this, people might fail several times but we should not quit trying. Like Edison said, "I didn't fail one thousand times. The light bulb was an invention with one thousand steps."

Nathan hit on my chest three times and said, "You should not quit. This is temporary. Someday, you are going to look back at this stage and you are going to smile. You will be proud of yourself that you passed this stage and you did it."

If You Have Something to Give, Give It!

Be kind whenever possible. It is always possible.

-The Dalai Lama

We saw the sun rising from the horizon. It was breathtaking to watch the gold and orange hues slowly scattering across the sky. I didn't look away from it. I wondered why I had never watched it before. Nathan looked at his latest version of the Apple Series 5 and said, "It's time for breakfast. Shall we go home?"

"Yeah let's go."

Then, the guy walking opposite wished us, "Good morning."

How on Earth does the word good exist with the word morning; I ignored him.

"Good morning," Nathan wished him back.

"Do you know him?" I enquired.

"Not personally, but we have seen each other twice or thrice," he answered.

"I'm really bad at this. I don't talk to people if I don't know them well."

"What's the worst thing that can happen when you wish a stranger 'good morning'? We are sending good thoughts. What's wrong with that?"

"Come, let's get some fresh vegetables on the way back," he continued and we walked towards the market, which was not that far. I thought mornings didn't have that much traffic; it was still the same as rush hour. Scooters, cars, autos were parked everywhere.

"Hey, I haven't seen you in a while," said a guy who came to us with parking tickets.

"Yeah, I was a little busy with my work. So, how are you doing? Your scar seems to be better now," Nathan said to him.

"I went to the doctor you suggested. He's a good doctor. Thank you for that."

"I'm glad I could help. See you again," and we left him.

"You guys seem close," I said.

"Yeah. When I first started my business with a small restaurant, I went every morning to the market to buy vegetables and parked my scooter here. So, we met every day. Sometimes, we even spoke about his life if we had some spare time. And, I get to know what happened with the scar on his face. So, I suggested him a doctor.' He replied.

"Why didn't you ask your employees to buy the vegetables? You are paying them, right?" I asked.

"I like doing it. I don't want to act like a boss. If it is something I can do, I'll do it no matter if it is anyone's job. I like meeting different kinds of people in the market."

"We went inside and it was a women's market. We passed through the busy stalls, loaded with fresh vegetables, fruits. On the other side, there were different kinds of fish. Everyone seemed to be in a hurry. The market is really a noisy place, all the hustle and bustle. Just then, a voice called from afar, "Why aren't you buying?"

We turned our back and it was a lady old enough to be my grandmother. We went to her stall and it was stocked with different kinds of local herbs.

"I have some," Nathan answered her.

"Take it whether you have it or not," and gave us a bunch of herbs.

Nathan smiled at her and tried to take out the money from his pocket, but the old lady refused to take it.

"I don't see the grandma that sits here," Nathan said.

"She has got cancer. She's not coming back," she informed us in a sad tone.

As we left the place, Nathan looked upset. "She always gave me extra lettuces, even though the price was high as fuck. I can't believe she has got cancer. I can't believe the extra leaves would have this much connection with her."

"Let's have some juice over there," he said, seeing the juice cart on the roadside.

It had all the seasonal fruits hanging and was attracting all the runners with those different- colored fruits.

"You have it. I don't feel like drinking it now."

"Why? It's good for your health."

"Well I can see, hear. So, I'm totally fine," I smiled and answered.

Nathan chose one of the fruits and turned to me, "Do you think that being able to sense these things makes you healthy? It's not only about the senses. A blind man can be healthy; a deaf man can be healthy. It's also about the mind and energy. Drinking juices in the morning helps you calm down your mind and help the body."

The guy passed him the juice and said, "thank you" and smiled at him.

"So, you keep smiling at the strangers huh. I guess smiling is your thing."

"Don't tell me you don't know the 'thank you and smile' therapy?"

"What is that?" I asked.

"What on earth were you doing all your life?" he asked me.

"Living my miserable life, I guess," I smiled and replied.

"So, tell me what is it?" I continued.

"Okay so 'thank you' has just two words, right? But, its impacts on people are huge. Some years ago, I was flying to Chennai to visit my sister. While I was going through the security check, for the second round right before I boarded the plane. I was asked to open my bag and the guy told me, 'So many books!'

I replied with a smile and said, 'Ok thank you.' 'Please go ahead,' he smiled back.

'Thank you for your service. You have a great day,' and we parted ways with a genuine smile.

It felt good. I boarded the plane in a good mood. I sat by the window and put on the headphones and was enjoying myself. I could see few college students trying to put their luggage in the overhead bins, which were already occupied by the Uncle; the newly married couple right behind me; the couple trying to hold their two kids together. I was seeing the normal chaos on a plane. I couldn't hear their voices but I could hear their sounds as I looked at them. Just then, I saw one of the flight attendants talking to a person right across me. I took off my headphones, and heard the lady saying, 'Sir, can you please delete that? It's prohibited'.

I guess the man was taking photos. The man replied and the conversation was going back and forth. At last, the photos were deleted. The lady thanked him with a smile. As soon as she turned away from him, in a nanosecond, I caught how frustrated she was. But, the moment she turned to another person, she was acting as if nothing happened. I realized some people are trained to smile for their job, no matter how fucked up they are feeling. So, in every possible way, thank the people who are doing a service. You are going to make someone smile, maybe for a second. It doesn't cost you anything. Love is everywhere. We think love exists in our close friends and family, but it is everywhere. The world is a happy place. If we are kind to people, they will give you the same kindness. Everyone is suffering, one way or another. Those two words are going to make them smile just for a second and lift their mood for a moment. Just say 'thank you' for their service. That guy wishing me 'good morning' was spreading love. I was also spreading love by wishing him back. He's going to have a great day and I'm going to have a good day, too. I did a good deed by suggesting a doctor to the brother who handles the parking tickets. In return, I received the kindness in the form of herbs. It's not about the things; I gave happiness for a few minutes and received happiness from another one. You can't make the whole world happy, but at least you can help one person smile for a moment."

Time Vs Money Vs Energy

Time abides long enough for those who make use of it.

-Leonardo Da Vinci

"Boss, here's my resignation letter," Phillips came to my desk.

I looked stunned and asked, "Why? Why are you doing this?"

'Boss it's the situation. I've been working overtime here; it's been almost three months you haven't paid me. I have to pay for my daughter's tuition fees and this is not working out," he replied.

I remained quiet for few minutes, and stared into his eyes. I could tell he was disappointed in me.

"I'm sorry for this," he told me.

"No, it's okay. I get it. This is something you have to do. Besides, I don't even have enough money to pay the rent. So, I can't even ask you to stop."

When something bad happened, the worse followed. I thought I could handle it but it was getting worse. I so wanted to make it work again. I wanted to live. I wanted to make everything right again. But, it wasn't easy. In fact, the worst was happening. It had been months I had paid my employees. My credit card bills were eating me alive. Maybe, I should take a loan or ask someone for money? Having no choice, I called a friend who worked in a bank.

"Hey."

"Hi! What's up?"

"Are you at the office? Can we talk?" I asked.

"Sure. What is it?"

"Listen, I need a favor. I'm having some financial problems. Can I take a loan from your office?" I asked.

"Loan? Sure. Come to the office and we'll talk it out" he replied.

"How much time does it usually take to process?"

"It depends on the type of loan. If you have your documents and your guarantor is ready, then it won't take long."

"Wait. Do I really need a guarantor?"

"Yeah. If you don't have a guarantor, we need proofs of assets, proofs of income, etc."

"Alright. Thank you for the information. I'll visit you soon." And, I hung up.

I neither had assets nor a person who could be a guarantor. So, this helpless guy called another one, "Nathan can we meet in the evening?"

"Evening? I have a meeting at 4, but we'll see. What is it?" Nathan asked me.

"No, I wanted to ask you favor."

"Okay. I'll try to make it."

After the call, I stared still at the red circle on the calendar in front and thought of the trips I had planned. When I was a young boy, all I ever wanted was to have a big house, a high-paying job and lots of money. So, I could travel the world, explore different cities and enjoy their food. I wanted to go to the famous diving spots, bungee jumping, to a *Coldplay* concert, visit the famous museums. I had the time and energy but not the money. And, I think I speak for most of us, about when we were young.

Now, when we are older, we still have the same dream but we don't have the time. In my case, I don't have the money either. But, some of you are lucky enough. You have the dream job and money. But, I bet you don't have the time to do all the things you wanted to do. You are caught up with life; you now have a family, so you can't quit your job to have your time. You work harder and harder so you can live the life you've dreamt of. But, now, look at you! You are above the age of 70, you have all the time, you have all the money but you don't have the energy to do all the things. Am I right? We won't question about this. Most of us will just accept this fact. like it's the code of conduct decreed by society. The problem with life is this.

The time on my watch read 5 pm. So, I went to the coffee shop Nathan and I had planned to meet. I looked at people, their attitude, how they run, how they talk, how they drink water, how they dress. The more I looked at people, the more I started asking all these answered questions.

'Why are we living for? Everyone is going to die someday. Why are we rushing for?' I was having an existential crisis.

Then, I saw the man in suits entering and walking towards me. My eyes delved into that person until he spoke, "Why are you looking at me that way?"

With a brittle smile, I answered, "You are lucky."

"Why do you think I am?" Nathan asked.

"You are just 31, and have the time, energy, and money. It's not common to have all three of these at one time," I remarked.

"If you are talking about that, then you are using the incorrect word. I'm not lucky. I made myself lucky. Success is never luck, man. Maybe three per cent luck, but 97 per cent hard work. Success is never accidental."

"I have time because I want to have time. Nobody in this world is always busy. They just like the fact that they are busy, even though they never admit it. They might be doing 9 to 5 jobs, but they still have 16 hours. As a human being, we need eight hours of sleep a day. So, again, they have eight hours left. The term, 'I don't have time' is for people who don't know how to manage time. And, let's say, if you are a super busy person, there's this law called the "Parkinson's Law".

For example, your boss gave you a project and she wanted you to finish it by next week. On the first two-three days, you might look into it but when do you actually finish the job? I can guarantee 80 per cent of the people will do it in the last two-three days before the deadline. In these two to three days, you'll work like crazy. It'll be like you've never worked like that before in your entire life. So, apply this law. For me, I wake up early and work for one or two hours in the morning like shit crazy. That will be half the work I'm supposed to do in the evening, so I have time for my family. Especially, for my daughter, because she is at that age where she is starting to know the world. So, we have to know her desires, what she is good at, what does she want in life and support her. If we do the contrary and suppress her potentials, she is going to lose in life. As parents, my wife and I, are trying the best we can do for her. Even though she is so busy with her work, she still makes time to bake cute panda breads in the morning. Sometimes, our daughter would ask for different shapes and sizes; she would ask her mom to make cartoon character cakes. And, my wife would watch videos the whole night about how to make cakes. She would even fall asleep with her phone. Sometimes, when I come back home exhausted and can't even speak properly, I find them building Lego houses together waiting for me; it changes everything.

With the technology growing fast, and as we are talking about 5G, it's so great that anyone can learn anything from the internet. But, some kids are so attached to the phones because their parents don't won't their children to cry or disturb them. It becomes a bad habit and they have become so attached that they can't live a day without the internet. So, the number of kids who love books are declining. It's a bad sign because everyone should have a reading habit. When it comes to us, I'm kind of old schooled. My wife built a cute perfect bookshelf for our daughter on her birthday and we make sure she has a reading habit because there is a lot she needs to learn from the books. And not just about learning, the books can find you peace; it can take you to certain places; books can be your best friend; they can help our lives become better. So, our daughter has a collection of books – from alphabets to the classic fairy tales – and we read to her. One time, I found the Harry Potter books on her bookshelf. I still don't know whether it is for the mother or the daughter. Just kidding! Anyway, we tried to teach her about the reality because the school system in our country doesn't teach these things. It teaches the kids to be brilliant, not intelligent. I recently saw on Instagram that 'If you are almost 22, you should have learned about the taxes in high school. First of all, Mitochondria is the powerhouse of the cell."

"That's it. If the kids are going to be a biologist or a biology teacher or something related to it, then it is necessary to know that mitochondria is the powerhouse of the cell. But that's just for per cent of the population. The remaining 98 per cent don't need to know the facts. We are in a reality. The kids need to learn about human emotions, how to handle finances, about careers, how to get up when life knocks you down. I mean the Pythagoras theorem does not apply to reality. I'm not saying I'm against the whole system because without it, I might not be able to read and write. That system brought me up, but our kids should learn more about the necessities of life. So, I have to be there for my daughter."

"And yeah energy, forget about old people just look at you! You look like you're going to die tomorrow. It's not surprising though. I mean, most people at our age don't have much energy. Why? In order to have the energy and keep a good health, we need to follow certain rules that we've been avoiding. We need a good amount of sleep; missing a few hours of sleep affects our energy level. Nowadays, we are so caught up with our work that our lives are filled with stress and anxiety. Well, we can't completely remove stress from our lives; However, we can minimize it. But, as it is common amongst us, we leave it that way.

We never think about taking proper care of our physical and mental health. We eat all the processed foods; it affects our energy level as well as our health. We need to eat a nutritious diet because our brain needs a steady supply of nutrients. If you are doing something you don't love, then you won't have any energy in your system. It's tricky sometimes, right? Well, there's a saying 'if you are doing something you love, then you'll feel like you are not working'. Or else, if you are doing something you hate, you won't have the energy even on the weekends or holidays. If you are doing a job you love, you'll have unlimited energy; no matter how hard you are working. To have unlimited energy, we need to have a good physical and mental health.

And for money, you have to be financially literate. I'll tell you things I learned from Robert. You have to know how to earn good money. You have to know how to manage money. We are at this stage, where our only aim is to earn money. Not everyone wants to be rich, but we do need money to survive. So, we only aim at one thing. But when will we have enough? When will we stop working? Enough money is not in the dictionary because the more money you earn, the more your expenses will increase. So, it's rare to find people who quit early and live a good normal life. For me, I plan to retire at 35 so I have 4 years left to work. When I say retire, I mean I'm not going to work anymore. How? You might think that I must have saved enough for 100 years, but no. I'm building my own empire, so that when I stop working, I'm still going to get good money coming into my account. So, you set up your own time, and plan to live financially free.

So, the key to a good life, no matter how old you are, is to figure out how to balance time, money, and energy all at once.

Money? No, Thank You!

The thing that differentiates man from animals is money.

-Gertrude Stein

"So, what is it you want to talk about?' Nathan continued the conversation.

I smiled and replied, "You're talking about retiring in a few years. Here, I am trying to make my ends meet. We are living so different lives.'

"Is something wrong?" he asked.

"I need some help. I've got some financial trouble. Can you help me out?"

"How much are we talking here?"

"50,000 will do it. I'll pay you back."

"Alright. I can give the money right now, but what about the next month? If you keep living like this, you are going to ask someone next month. At last, you wouldn't be able to get up. The famous saying of all time: 'Give a man a fish and you feed him for a day; teach a man to fish and you feed him for a lifetime'. So, I won't give you any money. Instead, I'm going to teach you how to earn money," he told me.

"Money! It's creating a big problem in our lives. I really hate money," I told him angrily.

"Yes, that's your problem, that's the start. That's the problem of the poor people. You all have the same mentality, that's why you are poor and are suffering. So, I joined a webinar and the guy was creating a poll about our relationship with money – like do you have a good relationship with money or an awful or awesome relationship? Then, an interesting thing caught me, his next words: 'Guys, it's going to be anonymous.' He knew if our names are shown on the screen, some people might not want to answer the question. That guy loves money, she loves money, it hurts their pride or I don't know. When I talked about money, people like you think I'm this greedy selfish person. You think money is the form of evil. Seriously? If you found a bag full of money, I'm sure you won't touch it because it's evil, right? If I wrote a whole book about it, most people probably won't read it saying they don't want to get rich. They just want to get rich spiritually. Funny! Yeah, go ahead if you are planning to become a monk. If you are planning to live a normal life, then you need money. I mean why are people afraid to admit they need money? Yes, you have to rich spiritually. But, when you don't have money to pay the bills, and your children are starving, how can you live a healthy life? I don't even agree with the fact that money is the sole reason for happiness because we've seen a lot of people with money living an unhappy life. What I want to say is money is also a part of our life. Before I had money, I started developing inner peace. When it was time to pay bills, all my positivity would disappear and I would start panicking at the end of the month. Because money matters! I knew panicking was not a solution. So, I figured a way to solve this money problem and I took it well, I guess.

"Tell me how to have money?' I asked him.

"What? I thought you hate money."

"I fucking hate it, but I need it. Tell me exactly how to get more money?"

'You know I drive a Mercedes, right? Do you know how I got it?"

"Yeah, you bought it with your frigging money of course."

"Well I bought with it. But, why a red Mercedes? Why not something else? I could have bought something, but why is that car mine? Because I wanted that and I didn't hate it. That's why it's mine. I have a great wife because I like her, so I approached her. If I didn't like or hate her, how the hell was she going to be my wife? So, you hate money, right? How is it going to be yours? The first step is the desire – not in a greedy way. You should stop thinking that money is evil. 'The love of money is the root of all evils', that's an old saying. Now, it's: 'Lack of money is the root of all evil'. You are now an evil person because you don't have money. You should attract them. Try to think of it as Marilyn Monroe, not like the white witch in Narnia."

Okay, so once you have attracted the money, you have it. Now, what? Is it going to stay with you forever? Of course not. If you don't believe me and you think that once you have money, it's going to stay with you forever, you can Google it. Hundreds of people will pop up. I saw a guy on Facebook, who won two million dollars some months back and is now homeless. So, if you don't know how to keep the money, it is going to be a problem."

"Tell me which brand of whiskey is your favorite?" he asked me.

"Well, there are a quite a few actually," I replied.

"I can say it's the expensive ones, right? So, did you drink it often when your business was at the peak?"

"Yeah, but not anymore. Now, I drink the cheapest whiskey in town."

"Why didn't you save the good whiskey? Why did you drink all of it? Why didn't you save the money to buy a good whiskey now?" he made a point.

He continued, "We have a neighbor, he works at a private company. I think he earns around 30,000 monthly. He made a decent living and after some years, he bought a van. I thought why didn't he buy himself a car instead of a van. But, then, he rented it and a few years later, I heard he had bought a piece of land. Again, after a year later, he built a small building and rented it. Year after year he did that; today, he owns four or five buildings. Now, he doesn't make a decent living. He is rich."

"But, what about you? Your business might be good and that leads to a good profit. But, the expenses will also increase. You will drink more expensive whiskeys. That is the problem with you guys. For example, let's say a guy has a monthly income of 30,000. If he is among a group of people, he will spend every penny saying 'who knows if I die tonight, life is uncertain, etc'. So, he spends all his money and doesn't die the next day. What now? Or, if he is among another group of people – the average people I should say. He lives in a rented apartment and his monthly expenses are around 20,000, including rent, taxes, food, etc. That leaves him 10,000. It is enough to buy the small things, or if he wants to eat outside. He wears a watch of around 6,000-7,000 by saving up for three months. His friend, who works in a bank, told him he can easily take a vehicle loan with his salary. He thought about it; maybe, someday when his salary would increase. But, he never thought why he didn't have a penny left by the end of the month. Most people don't think about anything, if the money is still enough to pay the bills, or there is extra to buy a watch or a car on loan. When his salary increases, he thinks 'well, I now have 50,000 salary. So, I'll have extra money at the end of the month'.

Did he? No.

That's when we say he is financially illiterate. When his salary increases, the guy who wears the a watch worth 6,000 would think of buying a TAG Heuer on instalments. This is because he thinks he has an extra 20,000. Do you think he must buy that watch? I mean it shows the same time, whatever brand you wear. What if something happens to you or your family? Are you going to sell your TAG Heuer and use the money? Is it going to be enough? No, right? So, he takes a loan. Now, his expenses increase from 20,000-35,000, including the loan and its instalment. It's going to keep going for years, no matter how much salary you get. It's never going to be enough because you are going to buy the things you actually don't need. You can always go to work with your scooter; you don't have to upgrade it to the latest Royal Enfield series if you don't have the financial security. See, buying your favorite watch is great, but I want you to know the timing. When do you buy that watch?

First, try to see the bigger picture and think about how to reduce your expenses with your extra 20,000. Forget the fact that your salary has been increased, and save the extra for some months or a year until you have 2 or 3 lakhs. Invest in something, so you can have an extra 10,000 flowing in your account; your monthly expenses are reduced to 10,000 from 20,000. Keep doing that for more months and finally, the extra income from your investment will take care of your expenses. Now, you have 50,000 extra per month. Forget about TAG Heuer, you can have your own watch company if you follow these steps. My mentor says getting rich is not about having these expensive shoes, watches, the number of cars you own. It's about the cash flow, how much money comes into your account. It's when your income is a lot more than your expenses."

"Is that it?" I asked

"No man. I'm just talking about money here. Alright, gotta go," he paid the bill and left in a hurry.

Rich people are all crooks?

My phone clock showed 4.30 am. I thought to myself, "Should I continue sleeping or should I wake up and do something?" It wandered for a moment and I couldn't bear the thoughts. So, I woke up. I put on my shoes and started walking out of the door. As soon as I hit the road, I wafted the breath coming out of my mouth. It smelled of a little mix of the cheap rum I had last night. Fuck! It was a cold foggy morning. Does it happen every morning or is it my luck? It was after years I was experiencing this. It changed dramatically; I guess 'climate change' is not a joke. I don't know what might happen to the next generation. I see a lot of young climate activists on social media these days. But, rich people don't care about these things. The only thing they care about is money. They don't care about the climate or the poor. They just don't give a shit about anything, except money. But, what can I do? Anyway, I passed by the market and it was something I didn't usually saw in the evening. I sat down on the park bench and looked around; there were people running back and forth. Some were trying hard to lose weight, while some to put something on their stomach. As I kept looking, I didn't see any poor people running. Maybe, the rich were the only one who wanted a healthy life, or are the poor people faking here as well? Maybe, the poor don't have time as they have to make ends meet. Then, among the rich people, I saw Nathan coming towards me. He was wearing a grey sweatshirt with a grey cap. I think he looked a lot younger than me, even though we were of the same age. When we picture or see a rich man, they usually look round, fat with greedy eyes. Looking at their belly, it's hard to tell whether they are pregnant or just fat. But, Nathan is different. He is tall and fit.

"A new watch, huh?" I asked, as he sat down beside me.

"Yeah, this is new. I love collecting watches more than anything. So, are you liking the morning atmosphere?" he asked me.

"It's too cold for me man."

"No, you'll get used to it."

"Yeah, but I think my bed is warmer; so, I prefer sleeping. And, seeing everyone here makes me ask serious questions to myself. I prefer alone, so I don't have to think about all this stuff."

"That's why I'm here. I'm here to answer all your unanswered questions. What is it?" he asked.

Then, we saw a guy and a girl come out of the car. They were all covered with branded clothes from head to toe. I could have paid rent with their shoes. Even the water bottle, the guy was holding, looked expensive. Then they took a few steps, started looking for a nice spot and started posing for photos.

"See, they are going to be like the #healthylife #morningvibe, etc. What a fake life! This is why I hate social media. Forget about them. All the couples acting cute on social media think themselves to be the 21st century Romeo and Juliet. In reality, there are so many things going on with their life."

"Then, don't follow them. Social media is actually a good thing; you have to know how to use it. Instead of following Instagram models, follow your mentors. For me, when I opened my account, all the things about life, positivity, not giving up, business tips, ideas would pop up on my timeline. That keeps me going, whenever I feel down. I learn a lot from these people. Every time I open my Instagram, I always learn something."

After a few rounds, the couple returned to their car and drove back.

"Nathan, do you know that going to the gym or taking a walk is for the rich people? They have to cut off the unwanted fats, which the poor try hard to gain. The lives of the poor sucks. The world is for the rich people. They can do whatever they want to do. They don't give a fuck about the people, the environment, the climate, the trees, the homeless, the social conflicts happening here and there. You know nothing, except for money."

He stayed silent, with his face looking down. He knew he was guilty because he was one of them. He was also a kind of thief, a scoundrel. Maybe, I preferred my life because I didn't wrong anyone. I was suffering alone. I'm not letting anyone suffer because of me, while I enjoyed my life.

"Do you know why I'm very focused on money? Do you know why I wanted to become rich?" he asked calmly.

"I grew up in a poor family. It was not that we had nothing to eat, but we were poor. We had a lot of debt. And, raising five kids was not a joke either. So, I grew up with people shouting at my mom, people who lent us money. I got scared whenever someone asked for my parents because I knew it was for money. I even encountered an incident, where they bought a gun to scare my parents; as a child, it hurt me a lot. I knew money was the problem. So, I wanted to earn many as I wanted to live financially free. As I grew older, as I started seeing the world, a lot was going on. So, I thought maybe I was selfish thinking about getting rich, while the whole world was suffering. Later, I realized it was okay to become rich. When I saw the old woman at the market begging, it hurt me a lot. I wanted to help, but I had nothing to spare for her. When I saw the children with the dirty clothes, sitting beside their mothers, who was selling vegetables, I wanted to buy clothes for them; but, I had no choice. When I saw the young boy working at the car workshop, I wanted to send him to school where he could learn about things, have fun with friends, worry about his homework, not with his life. See, there are two kinds of people in this world. Half are poor and half are rich. Seeing the poor people suffer, hurts me a lot within. But, what can I do when I can't even feed myself? That's when I realized I was not selfish; I wanted to become rich for the good cause. I wanted to help people and now I'm doing the best I can to help the poor. I'm possibly doing everything I could have. But, you are not wrong either. It's everyone's perspective about the rich people. Many rich people are like that, they don't care anything except for money. Sometimes, they even hurt the people, mess up the environment and forests. Some are liars, thieves, scoundrels polluting the air, water, and lots of other things. So, they are so good at this thing that they will contribute a little amount like 1 per cent of what they earn for the good cause. This is to make them look good and people won't question their wrongdoings. But, not every rich people is like that. I earn honestly. I tried really hard and I deserve this. And, it's not that I haven't thought anything about climate change, the social conflicts, and all these things. How can I be a part of it if my family is dying? I may sound selfish, but how can I let my family starve, while I raise my voice for the world? Everything begins from home, your family. If I provide enough for the family, I'm responsible. Then, I can raise my voice or, maybe become a part of the group. So, I plan to live financially free first and do all these things later."

The Rabbit Wins the Race

Do not wait to strike till the iron is hot, but make it hot by striking.

-William Butler Yeats

"Come on, get up. Let's take a walk," Nathan said.

"So, why did you and Daisy break up?" he asked.

"What? That's so random."

"So? I need to write down all the questions and set up the mood for each question?"

"Don't be sarcastic. No, it was a stupid fight. It's just that one thing led to another and all my insecurities conquered me."

"You are so stupid, man."

We kept on walking the path silently and I remembered Daisy. I had planned for a trip that didn't materialize. It was her birthday and I didn't sleep the whole night. I was so excited thinking about how happy she would be when she saw the tickets. It was quite a picture I painted inside my head. I got up from my bed early in the morning and set up everything. I took a cold shower and put on the best clothes I had, and waited for her just outside her house. She looked beautiful with her olive-green shirt; the thin color on her lips complimented her looks.

"Come. Let's celebrate."

She smiled and answered, "But I have some work to finish."

"Okay. We'll drop by your office first and I'll wait for you downstairs."

She sat beside me and I held her hand. It made me forget everything I was worrying about. We went for a really long drive with her favorite songs queued on the radio. All we had was just coffee, though the best one I've ever had in my entire life.

"Wait. Wait," I stopped her as we reached my place and closed her eyes with my scarf.

"What now?" she smiled and asked.

"You'll see."

I lighted the candles and cooked her stuffed baby pumpkin, a bowl of corn – her favorite food – and of course, my signature chicken. If I could keep these moments, I would put all of them inside a jar and bury it deep under the ocean.

As she was having her last bite of the cheesecake, I slid the envelope.

"What's this?"

"It's your birthday gift."

"What? There is more?" she opened it and reacted opposite to what I had in mind.

"Why? You know you are not in a good place right now financially. I appreciate everything you've done. Actually, I'm flattered. But, this is too much."

Now, the whole mood had changed. I had thought she'd be excited with it so I did it; to see her happy, but I guess she wasn't.

"I understand," I answered.

"No, you don't have to do this. Maybe, we can go on my next birthday or on your birthday or forget about birthday, we can go anytime. But for now, I don't think we should do this."

We had a really long fight that lasted for days. The thing about me was that I didn't want her to show that side of me. I wanted to feel like it's not that bad, I can do this. But now, it felt like she knew I was failing in life and it was something I couldn't take.

As I was in my series of thoughts, a guy bumped into me, "So sorry."

I didn't say anything to him; I just looked back at him, "Why is he in such a rush? Can't he walk slowly?" I murmured.

"Walking faster is a good thing you know. I like people who walk faster. I like people who know where they are going. Successful people walk faster than normal people in fact," he said.

"So, successful and unsuccessful people, the poor and the rich are different even when they walk? Huh! It's not a surprise though. How could the poor and the rich have the same lifestyle? The food we eat is not the same. The clothes we wear are not the same."

We kept walking until we passed by the small tea stall. "Should we have some tea?" I asked him.

"You have it, I just had a juice."

So, we sat down on the small bench at the corner. We saw the uncle pouring the tea into the glasses and I got up from my seat to get it. "Ah, this is nice. This is good tea," I said, as I took a sip.

"Have you realized you walked faster than the normal?"

"What? When did it happen?" I was surprised to hear that.

"Right now, when you were getting your tea."

"So? Should I walk like a turtle to get the tea that's in front of me?"

"Do you remember the famous story about the rabbit and the turtle?" he asked.

"Of course. The slow and steady wins the race. So?"

"The fast and steady wins the race in real. Now, the rabbit won, when he let go off his overconfidence and careless attitude. We need to walk faster in real. We need to run to what we want. Right before, when you were getting your tea, you walked faster because you knew where you were going. You knew what you were going to get. That is what I meant. We have to become the rabbit, with the right attitude because he is faster than the turtle. We breathe the same air, right? We drink the same water. It's not like we eat gold, while you eat grass. We both eat vegetables. You have the ability to walk faster, right? We both have limbs; so, it's up to you whether you want to walk faster or not. No one forbids you to walk faster. It is you who doesn't want to walk faster in life."

I read a story somewhere when I was a kid. Once upon a time, there was a man, the unluckiest man as he thought of himself. He thought of meeting the wise man, who lived in the mountain to seek some advice. He started his journey, and he met an old couple near to his house. They were farming and needed some help. The couple offered, 'We are too old to work on our own. So, if you help us, we can share the profit in half?'

The guy declined the offer saying, 'I don't have time for that. I have to meet the old wise man.' He continued his journey and finally, he reached. He told the old man about how unlucky he was and the old man said, 'Open your eyes. Luck is coming your way.' He thanked the old man and set on his journey back home. He met a man digging a piece of land. He asked, 'What are you doing?'

The man replied, 'I've hidden a pot of gold in this field. Now, I'm trying to find it.'

'You are going to dig up this whole field by yourself? It's pretty big.'

'I know. Can you please help? We'll share the gold 50-50.'

'Too bad, I can't help. The wise man told me to keep my eyes open as luck was coming my way.' And, he left the man in astonishment.

"We are in the 21st century, we can't be stupid. They say life is full of opportunities, one may go but another one will come. But, you have to grab it, no matter what, because thousands of people are waiting for that opportunity. You can't be too blind for this world. You have to run to it before anybody gets it. People are successful because they know what they want and walk faster to it, while you guys walk like the turtle."

I Said Confidence, Not Ego

"The most important thing is to build your confidence, not your ego. You have to look confident and be confident. Not just about business and clients, but about yourself. A person should be confident about himself. He should be confident when he speaks and about his looks. But, it's not a natural thing. You have to build it. The poor and the unsuccessful people destroy their confidence day by day and the successful people build it up day by day. In fact, the rich people don't always build confidence, they build their ego. I've seen and met a lot of people who are so full of themselves after they succeed in something. Whether black, brown, or white, male or female, poor or rich, successful or unsuccessful, people should not look down on others. You should not be full of yourself, and at the same time, you should have that confidence as a human being. So, a few months after I opened my restaurant, we hosted small events like acoustic nights, book reading, meeting the youths about the environment, and other small events. One day, we hosted a writer's meet. It was not a formal event. We just called some local writers and everyone interested in books. We put it on the Instagram pages, so interested people could come. There was this one guy. Nobody was wearing a suit except for him. Well, I'm not judging him on the dress, but it was a start. Everyone shared their journey and he was listening to every one of them. At the final moment, he stood up from his seat and came to the fore to share his writing journey. He remained silent for a few moments and looked at every one of us in the room and started talking. In the beginning, I listened to him. But, the mistake he made, was that he was wearing a suit to a writer's meet. Had it been a meeting for a start-up, I might have listened to him. He said, 'People should not dream.' I mean what the hell! Writers are dreamers. He also said, 'I stopped reading books because I know better than books.' I mean seriously? He told us he was a CEO; I checked him on Facebook, and yeah he was one. But, 'I'm the best' is not going to get you anywhere – whether a CEO or not. 'I know better than books' is not going to take you anywhere. We learn from books and learning doesn't have a stopping point. We should read as many books as we can. And not just about books, we can always learn something from everyone. We can learn from the kids, the poor, the rich. We can learn from nature, our surroundings. So, wherever or whoever we are, 'I'm not the best', 'you are not the best', 'we are not the best'."

"There is another totally different group of people. They think their existence doesn't matter to the world. Their future is so dark they can't see a thing. When asked why? They would make a bunch of stupid excuses like, 'I don't have friends', 'I don't have family', 'I don't have someone who loves me', 'I don't have money', 'my family is poor.' Hell no! You are worth it. You are born because your existence matters to the world. If your family is poor, mine was poor, too. If he/she left you, I was single for years as well. If you don't have money, earn it. Well, it doesn't grow on the trees, but if you plant a fruitful tree, you'll get the fruits; you can sell them and will have money. So, money does grow on trees. You are making an excuse for yourself. You are lying to yourself. If you think you'll die poor, you are going to die poor. If you think you can't find love, you won't find it. If you think you can't do it, you can't. If you think you can, you can. Stop giving excuses, build your confidence and start doing things."

Ningthou Phao Meitan Watle

There is no end of craving. Hence, contentment alone is the best way to happiness. Therefore, acquire contentment.

-Swami Sivananda

"Last, but not the least, let me tell you one important thing in life – contentment. If you don't know how to live a life with contentment, then no matter how wealthy you are, how successful you've become, you won't find happiness. There's a famous saying in Manipur, '*Ningthou phao meitan watle*'. The literal meaning is 'even the king doesn't have everything'. Have you come across people who actually say, 'I'm very happy with what I have? I have everything I want'. No, right? There are a few people, but most people are not contented with what they have. If we were born blind, the only thing we would dream about was the ability to see. If we were supposed to choose a million dollars and the ability to see, what would we choose? I would say keep your million-dollar and take everything I have, but please give me my eyesight. Fortunately, we can see, right? We were giving everything we have for this a few moments ago, and now why aren't we happy about it? Why are we taking this for granted and searching for more?

When we lack something, let's say we don't have enough money, we would forget about all the things we had and focus solely on money. And, if you don't know how to find contentment in life, you won't be happy with your life. You can't always have everything you want. You might get it now one way or other, but a few days later, you are going to want something more; it is going to continue. As human beings, we have a feeling called greed."

"I'll tell you a story. At the beginning, when I had started my business, I had a hard time like you were doing right now. I hardly had the money to keep the business going on. So, as I was eating lunch with my mom, I told her, 'Maybe, I should just quit everything and find a job.' That was coming from someone who hated working for other people. I was saying that because I was tired of everything. After lunch, I rode my bike to some work. The next thing I saw was an old woman sitting on the back of an auto, holding a large bag full of vegetables, and eating an ice- cream. Seeing the look on her face, I was moved. She was eating the ice-cream, as nothing else mattered in the world. She was living the moment. That made me realize I was over analyzing things. The poor, old woman may have children waiting for her to be fed. If she didn't sell the vegetables, her family might even starve. But look at her, she was enjoying her ice-cream. Maybe, sometimes, a good life is about sitting alone under a beautiful sky, eating an ice-cream, enjoying the moment and not worrying about anything, not giving a fuck about anyone or anything. This is what life is about. Life is simple. Even a pinch of salt can make your life tasteful. You don't always need exotic herbs or spices, just a pinch of salt. You don't need money right now, I didn't have the money back then, that doesn't mean I was starving. That's just a tiny problem, but we think about it as if it was the end of the world. I have friends and family who love me. I have a business, doesn't matter a good one or a bad one. After all, life is not that bad for me." Nathan told me.

"And, I also remember one time I went to the market. It was 10 years back. As I returned home, I caught an Auto and sat next to the driver's seat. I put on my earphones and looked at the crowded streets, trying to get back to the world. Just then, I heard someone calling and it was the guy who was driving the auto."

'How much?' he asked pointing at my watch.

"As I wasn't expecting he would ask the price of my watch, I answered him the time instead. He looked confused about my answer, so I corrected him."

"Then, he told me, 'Someday, I'm going to save enough and buy a watch like that'."

"That hit me hard. Earlier, I was jealous of people wearing expensive watches and felt bad about myself that I couldn't afford it. Meanwhile, some people were dreaming to buy my watch. Aren't we so selfish? I complained about the dishes, while others were trying to eat a small bite. I was disappointed about not having a Jordan, while some were trying to put a shoe on their feet. The future is uncertain, yet we feel bad for not having the luxuries. Why can't we be happy with what we have? Why do we always take the things we have for granted? This is so wrong. You live under a roof and sleep comfortably on your bed, while some look for a place to sleep on the streets. We are focusing on things we don't have, instead of focusing on the things we have. So, be happy with what you have. You see, one can't live a good life – no matter how rich or successful he is – if he doesn't know how to live with contentment."

"Anyway, I'm glad your thoughts have changed your mentality. They say, if you want to do something with your life, start by making your own bed. I'm happy you are trying to get up early. That's the start. These little changes matter in the end, that make you successful. Apply all the things I've told you before. That's how you win in life. It is that simple; it's just that humans make it so complicated.

You might not be fortunate as Ali Baba

But you can make your own Ali Baba

Things do not happen. Things are made to happen.

-John F. Kennedy

I made some toast for myself and ran out to work. I parked my old car and walked on the same road. It was a normal sunny day, but it looked different this time. I started noticing every detail on that street. I started wondering if the guy who was selling the phone covers on the street, the woman who was selling the vegetables next to him, and this guy walking the street had the same fate? Is fate even real? No, it's not. Fatalism is the thing I used to believe in, but not anymore. When something good or bad happens to us, most of us think it's all written and we can't change a thing. But, the truth is, we can change everything. It's not written anywhere. We make our own fate. Nobody has the right to do that. We are responsible for our past, present, and future. I'm going to make my own fate.

So, as soon as I reached my office, I sat down on the chair silently. I stared at the four-cornered wall that stood still and asked a lot of questions. 'Am I sad? Am I depressed? Why? What do I need? What kind of emotion am I feeling? Why am I living for? Do I have unfinished tasks before death?' I thought about so many things.

And, being a poor student academically, all my life I had a complex regarding this. I always felt bad about myself because I didn't know much. I felt disappointed whenever I saw or heard the 'know-it-all people' talk. I always admired them. But, does it really matter in reality? Do we ever find out the 'x' in real life? Knowing the specific dates in history, does it help us in reality? I lack money, but does anyone teach us about money at school? No, we were taught to get a job, right? So, the thing is I have to experience everything and learn it myself. Maybe, the people who have succeeded in life are the ones who have experienced a lot.

I always thought I was a very unlucky person. You know when I did something and failed, I blamed it on my luck. But, now, I understand why the big board that displayed the name of my company fell on a windy day. Everyone kept saying, 'What a bit of bad luck!' Nobody's board fell, except mine and I was depressed. It cost like 18,000 and at that time, it is a big amount.

It happened within a month of installing; it crashed and was crushed into pieces. It was supposed to be a one-time investment, and it was gone like that. After a few days, I went to take out some money from the ATM. People were standing in the line and I also joined the queue. Then, the machine got stuck. The lady next in line tried, but it didn't work either. One by one, they all tried, but none of their cards worked. Then, I heard a guy behind me saying, 'If one lucky person came in here, this machine would work.' It was my turn and it worked. So, the people were excited that the machine was working again. But, after I took out my money, the it stopped. I was the luckiest in there, whereas some days back I was the unluckiest. What I'm trying to say is in cases like these, we might call it luck. But, accepting myself as unlucky because the board fell, while nobody else does it, is wrong. It fell because it wasn't hung properly. That's why I was the unluckiest.

When we see or hear about a successful person, we can't say he/she is lucky. We don't see the struggle they went through to get there. I think luck is the output of the things we've done. We can't say a man is lucky, when he clears his UPSC exam. He is lucky because he worked hard for it. This is reality. So, I might not be lucky like Ali Baba to discover the secret cave, but I can make my own Ali Baba as Jack Ma did.

I decided to do something – to start something new. The moment I thought of that, a series of unanswered questions ran through my mind. But then I remembered my dad saying, 'whatever you decide you want to do, the first step starts with you. Forget about the business, you have to ask yourself why you want to become an actor, a musician, an engineer, or a doctor. Ask yourself why you want to do it? Ask yourself why you want to do that particular thing and why not something else? Everything should start with why and make sure you have an answer, or don't do it. If you are not clear about the why, then it's like getting on a boat and not knowing the destination; you end up rowing up and down the sea and you die. So, you should be very clear about your intentions. Are you doing this because you want to help people, or you want to build something that leaves your legacy or you are just doing because your friends are doing? And, when you have all your answers, do it then.'

And, I got my why.

Find Your Third Level

It was a Sunday afternoon. I got up from my nap and wanted to go out. So, I called my best friend.

"Are you free?"

"What's up?" he answered.

"You have taught me some things about life and I think I'm ready. So, let's celebrate. Let's have some beer."

"We can't celebrate, it's too early man. You have just learnt a few tips from me. You haven't done the hard part yet," he told me.

"I know but still, let's have a drink," I insisted.

"Okay, I'll be there in 20."

While waiting for him, I was browsing Facebook and saw a cover picture of the English textbooks of classes 11 and 12. Everyone was commenting, 'Aw miss my school days'. I was remembering my school days and we were crazy back then. Our English teacher was very strict, but I liked the way she taught. It felt like I'm in the story for real. I remembered one chapter; I had gone to him because I had a lot of questions. Some of you might have read this story before, *The third level*, if you're a CBSE student. It was about a man who thinks the Grand Central station has three levels, but nobody, including his wife, believes him because there was no third level in real. Then, he talked to his psychiatrist friend who told him that the third level is his medium of escape from the reality, his insecurities, worries, and fears. Back then, I understood the story but was too young to understand the man. I thought he was crazy. But, as I grew older, I started knowing him more. In fact, everyone is not aware that we have our own third level. Nathan talked about so many things about positivity, but I'm sure he knows these things because he has also felt the negative things. And not just him, a man knows happiness because he knows what sadness is. Virginia Woolf asked 'how many times have people used a pen or paintbrush because they couldn't pull the trigger?' Thousands of people! This is life, things happen and they are going to happen. Nathan might have taught me about life, but he is not a God. He is a human being with emotions after all. He doesn't have a switch that can be turned on and off to his likings. He just taught me how to how to handle it.

I remember when the COVID-19 pandemic hit the world and the government shut off everything, and we weren't allowed to go outside. We were hearing news of the people testing positive. Everyone was afraid and we were turning on the news 24*7 for a miracle to happen. All the telephone lines were busy because people were calling their relatives and friends; it was a mess. My mom asked me for a hand to get the sewing machine from the storeroom. 'Everyone was panicking and she was in the mood to sew a cloth?' I thought. Now, I know that her old, rusty sewing machine is her third level. She was escaping from the reality for a while. Now, I know why my sister uses her paintbrush when something troubled her. I wondered what made people write books? Maybe, because when they are lost in the world, they just want to escape from the reality with their pen and paper. When my brother broke up with his girlfriend, the house was reverberating with the sound of his drums. Some travel the world, some read, some sing and that's how we live. That's how we stay sane, no matter how hard life knocks us down. We need to find our own third level, our medium of escape.

His Laws of Life

-Everything starts in the family

One thing I realized is that everything starts in the family. After the fight I had with my brother, I was totally cut off from everyone. I thought my family hated me and I hated them. I thought I was just a pain in the ass to them. They had been trying to talk to me, but I had been ignoring them for months. I guess, I was just angry with myself. I don't hate my family. Hate is a big word. And, if you hate someone, you are torturing yourself. Because when you hate someone, it means you have a strong negative emotion about him/her and you will keep reminding him/her every day in a bad way. It's going to leave a negative impact on you. And, you are wasting your precious moment with that negative energy. Why would anybody do that? When it comes to family, they are going to be there for you. They are going to support you. Even though we were born and raised by the same mother and father, we have so many differences. It's just that we have the same physical appearance, but our thoughts are so different; it often leads to fighting.

What I should have done with our differences is that I should have learnt from them. From my eldest sister, I should have learned to be bold and how to stand up for myself. Though a kind-hearted, positive person, she knows how to draw a boundary for herself so that nobody takes an advantage of her. She doesn't let anybody take her for granted. And, from my other sister, I should have learnt patience. You know, being a human being, she must have felt angry or sad, but she would never put it out. You will never hear anybody talking bad things about her because her patience level is so high that she can keep everything under control. From my elder brother, I should have learned how to be responsible. You won't believe what a workaholic he is. He loves his job and taking responsibility. Work matters to him. I should have learnt from him that I need to work hard to achieve what I want in life. I need to take responsibility for my work. And the other brother – he is the nicest human being ever. He is the most loyal person I've ever met in my life. Sometimes, we get frustrated that he thinks too much of other people. But, it's a great thing he is like that and I should have learnt loyalty from him. I learnt how to think of others, how to love others despite everything. And, what about me? What am I good that? I'm a risk-taker. Though once I was afraid of failure, I still took a risk and did something I wanted to do. I'm the one who never quits. So, whoever I want to become or whatever I am as a person, I should apply these things I learned from my siblings. Being bold, patience, responsible, loyal, and a risk-taking attitude. First, you have to be bold in whatever you do; you have to be brave enough to tell the world what you feel. Second, you also need patience; in business, there are going to be lots of up and down, and you need a high patience level. The third one is you have to learn to take responsibility. You need to work on what you want. In work, you should not blame anyone for your actions. In life, too, you have to take responsibility. The fourth one, be loyal. Be kind to your family, friends, employees and juniors. And the last one, learn to take risks.

Au Revoir

"Okay, where do you want to go?"

"That place where you met me by the cliff."

"Yeah, I wanted to have a beer over there that day," he said.

"Okay, let's go!"

We packed the back of the car with food, a couple of beers, and drove off. That trip is still my favorite. When I think of that, it gives me the chills – the good kind. I didn't know we were driving for hours, until I saw more trees than the big buildings. The closer we get to the destination, the greater view we had. I lowered the window and could feel the smell of the fresh air; the sound of Radiohead in the background. I was so engrossed in that moment. I felt like I was in a movie or a music video. I looked at my best friend, he smiled at me and our eyes did the talking. It was my escape from the reality. For the first time in years, I was actually enjoying my present.

We both felt the silence for a while. We both felt the wind blowing through us. We sat on the same spot; I didn't see much change with everything surrounding me. The only thing that changed was me. The trees looked the same, the sky was still the blue, the silent breeze, the sound of the birds singing in different tunes. The sun was still looking big and bold. It was beautiful. Am I realizing this just now, or did I see this the first time I was here? I guess we are too blinded sometimes, if we focus only on the bad things.

"It's nice. Sometimes, I take a break like this. We can break the cycle sometimes. I took a day off and went alone to have a good time myself because alone time is very necessary. I heard someone said, 'You were born alone. Not with your wife, your children, your brother, your sister, or gold, silver, diamonds; you were born alone, naked, without anything. And, you were going to die the same way – without anyone or anything. So, love yourself and take care of yourself first. Hence, we should take a day off sometimes to relax and have some 'alone time'.

The smell of the clean air, the quiet sound of nature, with no cars to disturb. Everything is beautiful if we look at it beautifully. Even the water sloping its way down is beautiful. I also realized that the higher we go, the better the view of the world we see. Life turns out to be simple.

Aristotle Onassis said, "It is during our darkest moments that we must focus to see the light." Nathan was the one person who guided me to see the light. We stayed quiet; we looked straight at what was in front of us. I wished if I could stop the time for a while and stay there longer. We can't do that because every moment has to pass, whether it is good or bad. The world will keep changing but don't worry; we have the power to make moments that are better than this beautiful moment.

"Are you going home? Where are you going?" I asked.

He smiled and said, "Inside your head. You know I'm not real. I don't exist. You are Nathan. I'm you. I'm the positive version of you and you are the negative version of yourself. It's all happening in your head. My wife, who you keep talking about how great she is, is Daisy. You let her go that easy because you were focusing on the negative things in your life; you didn't see the greatness in her. My daughter, whom you think is the cutest, is going to be yours if you start acting now and change your mindset. The beautiful red Mercedes I drive is the one in your head you wanted a long time back, but were too lazy to work for. The businesses you thought I owned are the things you wanted in your head, but didn't know how to do it. All the things I've told you or taught you are already known. It's coming out of your head. Even though you knew it, you needed someone to tell you these things. That's why I'm here with you. It's just that you are too blinded by your negative perspectives of life that you don't see it. They are all yours, but you have to change. If you keep doing what you were doing, this is the life that you get. The life you deserve. I've told you in the beginning that it's all in the mind. You are playing these all in your head. Now, you know what to do. So, get up and start doing it. Believe in the power of now. You are everything, you can do it."

Tears started rolling down my eyes and I realized the whole thing. I saw Nathan getting up from his seat and I saw him walking away from me slowly; he disappeared in front of my eyes.

"Hey!" Daisy looked surprised to see me.

"I got you these," and I gave her the flowers.

"Thank you. How are you doing?"

"I'm good. Great, actually. By the way, you look great."

"Thanks."

"So, you have some time? Can we grab some coffee?"

"Sure."

The way she looked at me before getting into her car, I knew I was okay. So, I drove behind her car. I still fought with my gear, but this time it was smoother.

Just then, my mom called, "Hello!"

"Are you driving?"

"Yes."

"Then, call me back later."

"Wait. Wait. I'm coming home this weekend, so cook something nice for me," I was smiling at myself thinking 'now I'm officially happy'. I came back to life.

It started drizzling when we were about to reach the place. I guess mother Earth was in my favor. She sure knew how to set up the mood. We parked the cars a few meters away from the place and saw the clear warm light of the cafe from a distance. There were small lamps leveled with the winter gem boxwood on the sideways showing the way to cafe. The windows were open to get the fresh scent from outside. The specials were written on a blackboard with chalk. The flowery aroma and the musty smell combined to form one hell of a scent.

"Wow. This place is amazing." And, her smile. It was the most beautiful thing I've ever seen.

"You like it? Come, I'll show you around."

We sat down at my favorite spot next to the book shelf, where we saw the raindrops drizzle down the glass window; we could see the beautiful trees in the front and the mountains afar. We had clear lights on each table, but she shone the most. And the great part is, the coffee is free at my cafe.

You might have heard of this before, "Behind every successful man, there's always a woman." For me, it is the woman sitting next to me. I might not speak for everyone in this world, but I think some people can understand. In the famous book, *Think and grow rich*, it says, "The emotion of love, in the human heart and brain, creates a favorable field of magnetic attraction, which causes an influx of the higher and finer vibrations afloat in the ether."

My mind works the best when I'm in love. To me, love is such a beautiful feeling in the world. We survive because of love; we stay because of love; we live because of love.

They say love may not make life easier, but it does gives meaning to life. So, whenever someone asks me what is life? I would answer "Love someone, and you will know life."

Love is the thing that keeps us going and feeling alive. It's just a four-letter word that makes a difference to the world. It lets you see how beautiful the world is. I believe in love. And, I don't believe there is such thing as true love, because you either love someone or not. There is no such thing as true.

The first day I met her, I never knew I would fall for her. And, she felt the same. She is the strongest woman I know, with the prettiest smile. When I met her, I wondered why she was like that. Why did she suffer so much? Why would people hurt her? Why is she angry inside? Why is there so much pain? The answer is she is too kind for this world. She doesn't ask for more, she just wants the person with the same wavelength. We both were a mess actually, we still are. But, we are in love. I don't know if I believe in the idea of a soul mate, but I do believe that everyone is perfect for someone. When I say perfect, it doesn't mean falling in love like they do in movies. Perfect means you understand each other, give each other space, don't cheat, work on your problems alone, and if necessary, work it out together.

Someone who thinks like you or maybe different but supports you. Someone who shares her happiness and sadness with you. And, when you love someone, you should not take her for granted. John Lennon said, "We've got this gift of love but love is like a precious plant. You can't just accept it and leave it in the cupboard, or think it's going to get on by itself. You've got to keep watering it. You've got to really look after it and nurture it."

And if love is there, you witness magic. You should not give up that easily.

The sun shone bright through the window and my eyes looked at every corner of the room. I woke up next to the love of my life, and it was Emma's first birthday. We had a cake made by her mom.

"Run, Harold run! Your mother is going to hit you. Run!" I laughed, as I held my one-year old daughter in my arms. My wife was running after our son.

"Come here, you!" Daisy continued chasing him inside our huge living room. I was sitting on the couch and my eyes were on the 146-inch TV.

"I'm sorry. I won't do it again mom," Harold said, as his circled around the couch I was sitting.

"Harold, stop running. You're going to spill the juice on the rug. Stop!" Daisy continued chasing him.

Then, I held Harold and I told her to stop, "Honey, he said he's sorry."

She stopped and stared at him, with those angry brown eyes; he winked at her.

"See, he's doing it again," my wife said, as she tried to get Harold's ear.

I caught her hands and held her in. And, it was my home, with three of them lying on my chest silently.

17 Years Later…

I walked into Harold's closet and chose a green shirt because it is his mom's favorite color. She is a great woman, who has a sense of beauty in things. She is a perfectionist unlike me, who would nod at everything. It's like we are the living proof that says 'opposite attracts'. We looked into the mirror and saw the reflection of a guy in neat clothes. Everyone used to say he is more like his mom, but when I saw the reflection, he is like the younger version of me. And, I told him, "Harold, you can make a lot mistakes but when it comes to dressing, be like Barney, suit up."

He asked, "What do you mean dad?"

I answered, "Have you heard people saying, 'Don't judge a book by its cover'? It's one of the famous saying. When you go to a bookstore and browse books, you pick the ones based on their covers, right? When we see someone or meet someone, we can say a lot about them by the way they dress. "The first impression is the last impression."

The first impression is very important; it's the first thing people notice about you. Before you start the conversation, they see how are you dressed and how do you look. I'm not saying you have to wear suits all the time or wear only branded clothes. It's not about what kind of clothes you wear; it's about how you wear it. For my case, let's say, I'm going to meet a client and I go there looking like a homeless person. Do you think I'm going to work with him? When it comes to meeting the clients, investors, and everyone, you should give them a good first impression. So, you have dressed up for it."

"And, that's the start son. I'm going to teach you everything I know about life. Life is a beautiful journey, but if you don't know how to walk, you are going to stumble."